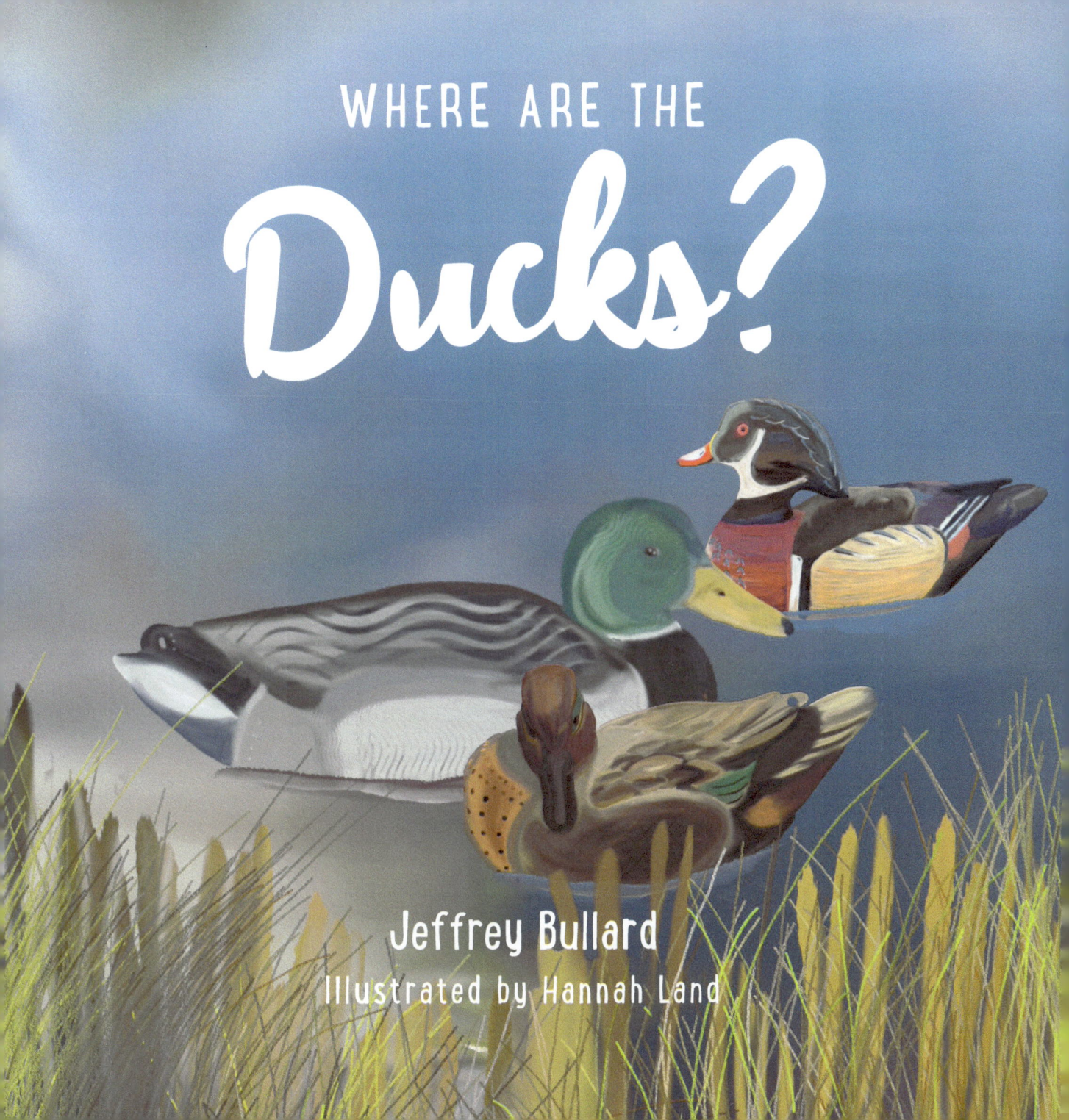

Where Are The Ducks?
Copyright © 2022 by Jeffrey Bullard

All rights reserved. No part of this publication may be reproduced, distributed, or transmitted in any form or by any means, including photocopying, recording, or other electronic or mechanical methods, without the prior written permission of the author, except in the case of brief quotations embodied in critical reviews and certain other non-commercial uses permitted by copyright law.

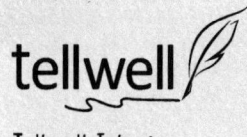

Tellwell Talent
www.tellwell.ca

ISBN
978-0-2288-7410-2 (Hardcover)
978-0-2288-7284-9 (Paperback)

WHERE ARE THE
Ducks?

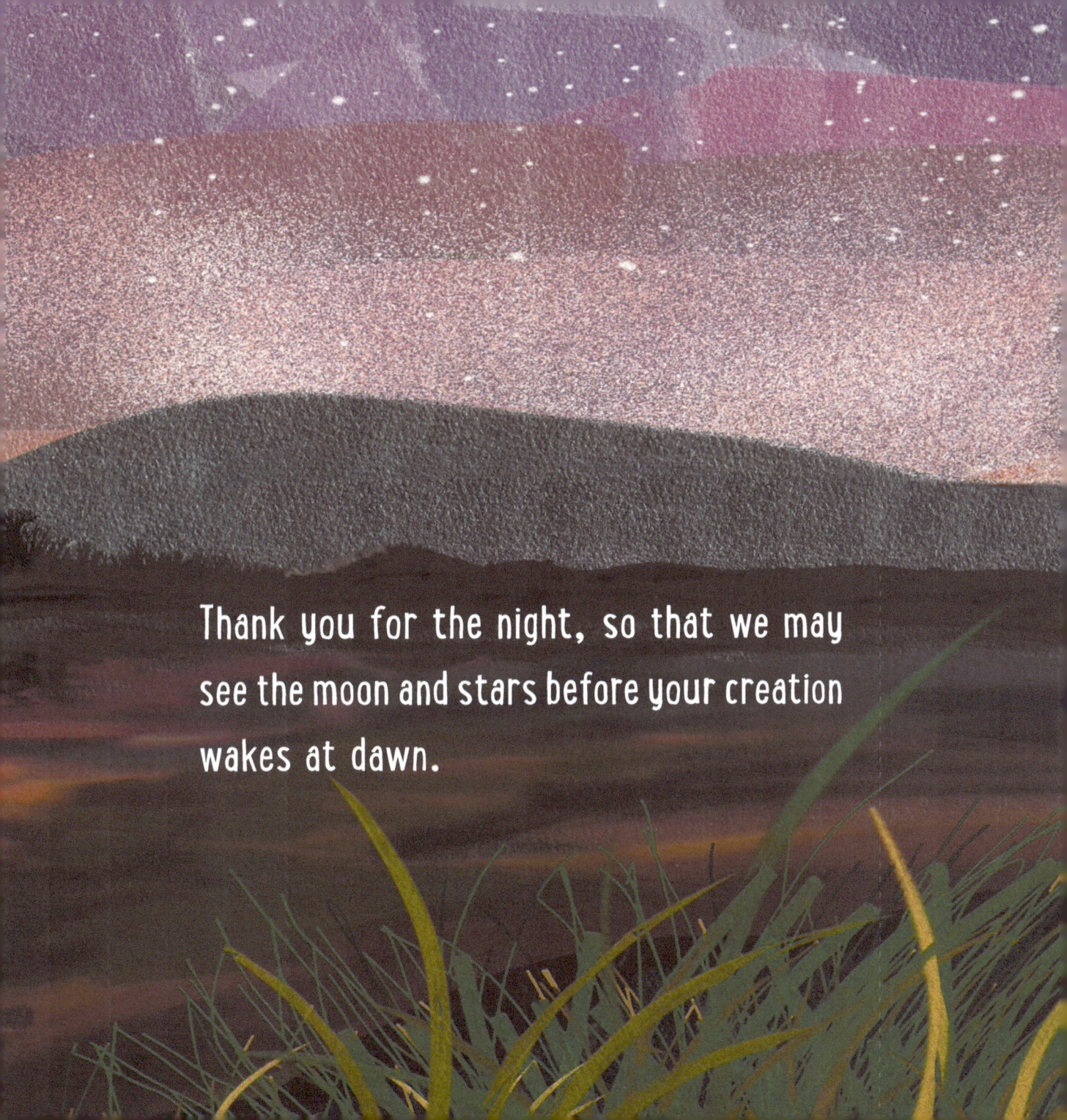
Thank you for the night, so that we may see the moon and stars before your creation wakes at dawn.

The geese honk, "wake up!" like choirs in song.

But where are the ducks?

The turtles stretch out their necks and yawn.

The blackbirds move in a mighty throng.

But where are the ducks?

The beavers go to work, swimming strong.

Eagles ride the wind with grace and calm.

But where are the ducks?

But where are the ducks?

Ducks! There are the ducks,

Waiting for more ducks to come along.

ABOUT THE AUTHOR

This is Jeff's first children's book, inspired by days and days of looking for ducks but only seeing many other wonderful creations. Jeff studied Classical Music Composition and English Literature, but he mostly loves jamming on a bass guitar and being in the outdoors any chance he can. He is devoted to God and his family. Jeff is married to DeeAnn and is the Dad of Jessie and Jacob and the Popi to Silas and Shepherd. He and DeeAnn reside outside of Sherman, Texas.

ABOUT THE ARTIST

Hannah is a small-town artist who works primarily in digital art platforms, ink, and acrylic paint. Her signature art is done on denim fabric. Hannah first began illustration with the hopes of creating visual stories about her children to capture the memories of their childhood.

Milton Keynes UK
Ingram Content Group UK Ltd.
UKHW050737030124
435384UK00003B/7